For Isabelle, Joey, Iona and Callan

First published 2021 by Macmillan Children's Books
an imprint of Pan Macmillan
The Smithson, 6 Briset Street, London EC1M 5NR
Associated companies throughout the world.
www.panmacmillan.com

ISBN: 978-1-5098-6661-8 (HB)
ISBN: 978-1-5098-6662-5 (PB)

Text and Illustrations copyright © Jessica Meserve 2021

The right of Jessica Meserve to be identified as the author and illustrator of this work
has been asserted by her in accordance with the Copyright, Designs and Patents Act 1988.

1 3 5 7 9 8 6 4 2

A CIP catalogue record for this book is available from the British Library.

Printed in China.

MACMILLAN CHILDREN'S BOOKS

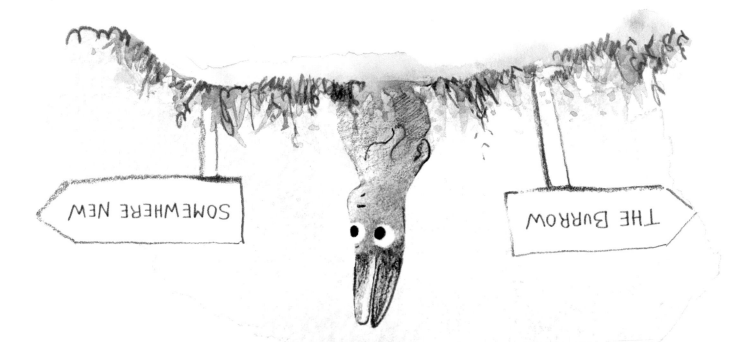

SOMEWHERE NEW

THE BURROW

BEYOND THE BURROW

JESSICA MESERVE

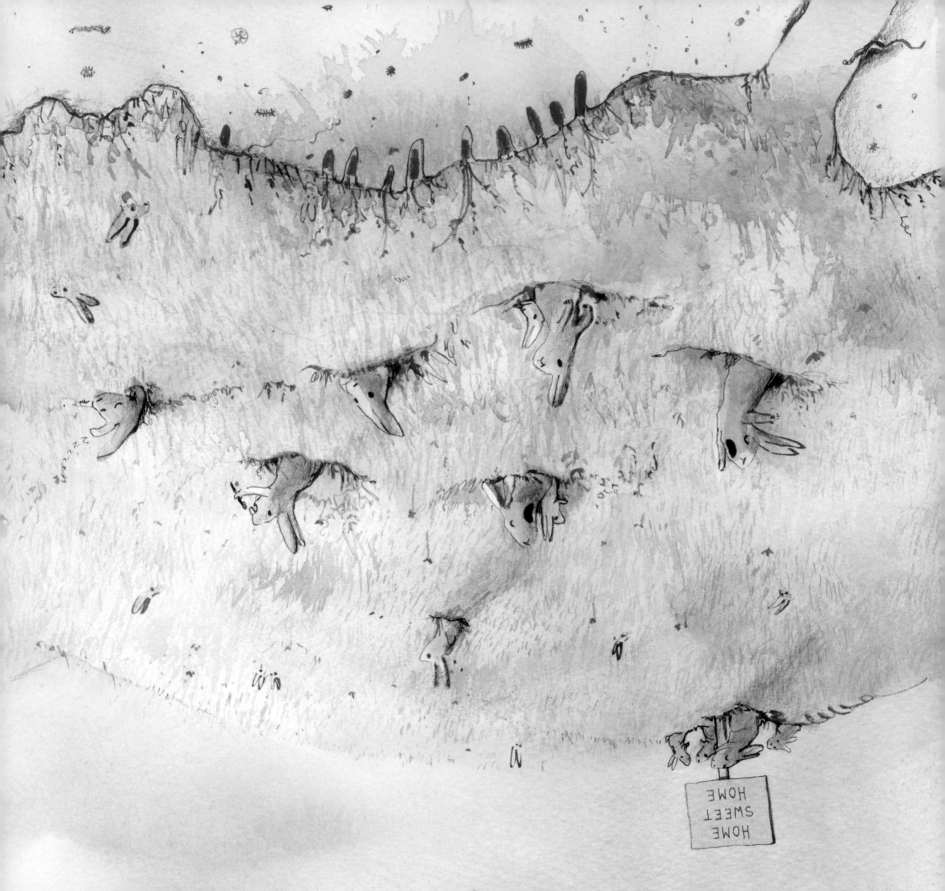

Rabbits love staying close to home.

And home for a rabbit is a burrow
where it is warm and safe and cosy.

Rabbits like to live with other rabbits.

HOME
SWEET
HOME

In fact, rabbits are extremely suspicious of anything that is NOT a rabbit. Especially things with feathers, scales, horns or hooves. They are particularly wary of anything giant, clawed, hairy and scary.

Psst! What about me!

I like to eat bugs!

PRACTISE
DIGGING
TWICE A DAY

STAY CALM
AND EAT
CARROTS

Rabbits stick to what they know, and as well as loving home, and hopping, they also adore carrots.

One morning, Rabbit
found the sweetest carrot,
perfect for breakfast.

It was only a whisker
out of reach.

She stretched one little paw,
just beyond the burrow.

Then two . . .

Then four . . .

Until . . .

She tumbled,
and rolled
and fell . . .

WATCH OUT!

UNKNOWN
AHEAD!

LAST
WARNING!

... down the WRONG hole!

Falling is NOT a very
rabbity thing to do.
In fact, it's something
of a disaster.

It isn't warm,
it isn't safe
and it certainly
isn't cosy.

And just when
Rabbit thought
things couldn't
get worse ...

BEWARE
THE
NOT-RABBITS

POINT
OF
NO RETURN

... they did.

Getting wet is
NOT a very
rabbity thing
to do.

Nor is holding
your breath.

Or clinging
to a log.

But this little rabbit didn't have much choice. She clung on tightly until finally she came to a stop, far, far beyond the burrow.

SOMEWHERE NEW!

"At least I haven't met anything that is NOT a rabbit," she thought.

And this not-rabbit was giant and clawed
and hairy, and almost certainly scary.
But Rabbit didn't wait to find out.

But then she did.

She did the only rabbity thing she could.

She hopped . . .

and she dug . . .

"What if the not-rabbit
is hungry too?" she thought.
"What if it eats ME for breakfast?"

Rabbit's paws ached
and soon her tummy
started rumbling.

This was not at all
like home! It was
cold and damp and
frightening!

. . . and she hid.

But it didn't.

In fact, it left something behind.

It was NOT a carrot.

Rabbit was very suspicious.

But she was very, *very* hungry.

She took one nibble . . .

It was the most delicious
thing she had ever tasted!

Then Rabbit had a very new
and very bold thought.

"Maybe not-rabbits
and not-carrots
are okay after all!"

But how could she
find out for sure?

Just then, she heard strange sounds coming from above.

Rabbits are not usually brave and they don't usually climb.

But it *had* been a non-rabbity kind of day.

So up Rabbit went . . .

...and when she reached
the top she said,

"Thank you!"

"You're welcome!" said the
not-rabbit.

It was giant, clawed and
hairy, but not so very scary.

There were other not-rabbits in the trees too. Some with horns and hooves, some with beaks and feathers, and others with fur, teeth, scales and tails!

They all gave her the warmest of welcomes. They even offered her their favourite snacks! So Rabbit did something kind in return.

She showed them how to hop. Some of them were quite good at it!

Then, feeling much
braver, Rabbit tried
hanging . . .

swinging,

camouflage,

dancing,

and even flying!

Now this *could*
have been a
disaster . . .

. . . but it wasn't!

"Falling," thought Rabbit, "is fun when you know there's a soft landing."

That night, Rabbit couldn't sleep.
She thought about home and how
much she missed the burrow.
It felt so very far away.

"Will I ever find it again?"
she wondered.

But as the sun rose,
she spotted a familiar
hill shining in the distance.

And now a much, much braver
rabbit decided to head for home.

She wasn't sure how
to get there.

The journey was long . . .

and difficult.
But . . .

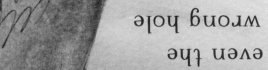

was less scary

... even the
wrong hole

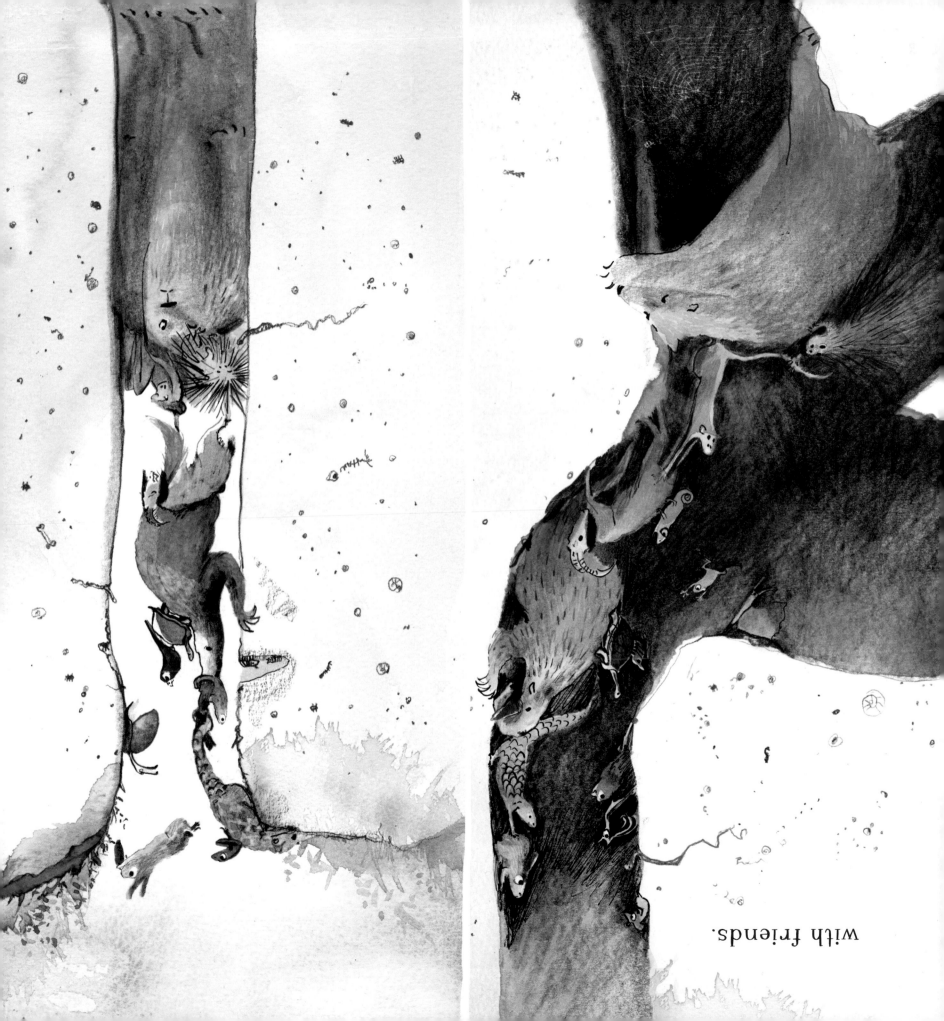

with friends.

As Rabbit led the way, bounding towards
the burrow and the sweet scent of carrots,
she thought things couldn't get any better.

LOTS OF
FUN AND
ADVENTURES
THIS WAY

NEW HOME

But they did!